THE HUNGRY BROTHERS

BY JOHN MEJIAS

WHAT ARE YOU TWO DOING?

WE'RE
MAKING
ART!

WHAT'S IT FOR?
HUH?

WHAT ARE YOU GOING TO DO WITH IT?
HMM

WHY ARE YOU MAKING ART?

BECAUSE WE'RE

HUNGRY

WE HAVE
TO MAKE ART

HUNGRY

WE
CAN'T
NOT
MAKE
ART

WE
MUST
MAKE
ART

HUNGRY

BECAUSE
WE'RE
HUNGRY

HUNGRY

UM, DO YOU WANT A SANDWICH?
NO THANKS

ISBN: 978-0-9798841-1-5

FIRST EDITION

PRINTED IN CHINA

BOOK DESIGN
BY JOHN MEJIAS

FOR MORE INFORMATION:
WWW.4NPUBLISHING.COM